# DK READERS

## Level 1

## Level 2

# A Note to Parents

DK READERS is a compelling program for beginning readers, designed in conjunction with leading literacy experts, including Dr. Linda Gambrell, Professor of Education at Clemson University. Dr. Gambrell has served as President of the International Reading Conference, National Reading Conference, and College Reading Association.

Beautiful illustrations and superb full-color photographs combine with engaging, easy-to-read stories to offer a fresh approach to each subject in the series. Each DK READER is guaranteed to capture a child's interest while developing his or her reading skills, general knowledge, and love of reading.

The five levels of DK READERS are aimed at different reading abilities, enabling you to choose the books that are exactly right for your child:

**Pre-level 1:** Learning to read
**Level 1:** Beginning to read
**Level 2:** Beginning to read alone
**Level 3:** Reading alone
**Level 4:** Proficient readers

The "normal" age at which a child begins to read can be anywhere from three to eight years old. Adult participation through the lower levels is very helpful for providing encouragement, discussing storylines, and sounding out unfamiliar words.

No matter which level you select, you can be sure that you are helping your child learn to read, then read to learn!

LONDON, NEW YORK, MUNICH,
MELBOURNE, AND DELHI

**For Dorling Kindersley**
**Project Editor** Heather Scott
**Designer** Hanna Ländin
**Managing Editor** Catherine Saunders
**Art Director** Lisa Lanzarini
**Publishing Manager** Simon Beecroft
**Category Publisher** Alex Allan
**Production Editor** Clare McLean
**Production Controller** Poppy Newdick

**For Lucasfilm**
**Executive Editor** Jonathan W. Rinzler
**Art Director** Troy Alders
**Keeper of the Indycron** Leland Chee
**Director of Publishing** Carol Roeder

**Reading Consultant**
Linda B. Gambrell, Ph.D

First published in the United States by
DK Publishing, 375 Hudson Street,
New York, New York 10014

10 11 12 10 9 8 7 6 5 4
DD545—07/09

DK books are available at special discounts when purchased in bulk
for sales promotions, premiums, fund-raising, or educational use.
For details, contact:
DK Publishing Special Markets
375 Hudson Street
New York, New York 10014
SpecialSales@dk.com

A catalog record for this book is available
from the Library of Congress.

ISBN: 978-0-7566-5525-9 (Paperback)
ISBN: 978-0-7566-5524-2 (Hardcover)

Color reproduction by MDP, UK
Printed and bound in China by L-Rex

Discover more at
**www.dk.com**
**www.starwars.com**

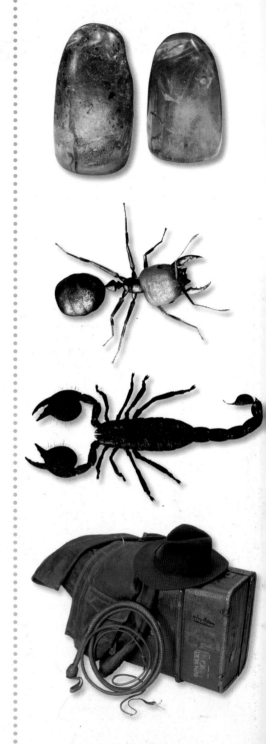

# DK READERS

BEGINNING TO READ

1

# Indy's Adventures

Written by Lindsay Kent

Doctor Indiana Jones is an archaeologist. His friends call him Indy.

He teaches at Marshall College. Indy also travels the world searching for ancient artifacts.

His journeys are often very dangerous. Shall we learn about some of his adventures?

Indy always
takes his
whip on
his travels.

It has helped him escape from lots of tricky situations.

Indy wears a special hat. It is called a fedora.

Indy travels on foot and by car
and by plane.

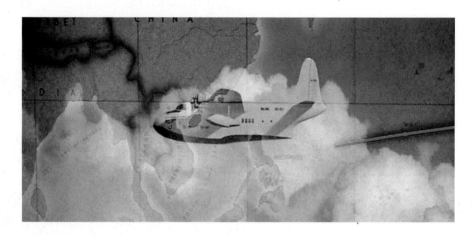

He also travels by horse.

Indy even rides on an elephant!

Sometimes his trips don't go
as planned!

On one trip, Indy nearly gets
squashed by a tank!

On another trip, Indy and his friends have to jump out of a plane on an inflatable raft.

What a lucky escape!

Indy looks for objects that are
very valuable. Other people want
to find them, too.

Some of the people are dangerous
and will do anything to find
the objects.

On one adventure, Indy must find the Sankara Stones.

They have magical powers.

The stones have been stolen
from a village in India.

Indy goes to Pankot Palace to
find them.

A bad man called Mola Ram has stolen the Sankara Stones.

He makes Indy drink a potion that puts Indy into a trance.

Indy's friend, Short Round tries to wake him up from the trance.

Indy gets angry, but then he wakes up from the trance.

On another adventure,
Indy searches for the Ark
of the Covenant.

The Ark is very powerful.
It is buried in a desert in Egypt.

Belloq is Indy's enemy. He is trying to find the Ark, too.

Oh no! Belloq traps Indy in a room filled with snakes!

Indy is afraid of snakes.

He has been scared of them since he was a boy.

He uses a flame to keep the snakes away.

Indy's father is an
archaeologist, too.

He is searching
for the
Holy Grail.

The Holy Grail is
a goblet.

It can make
people live forever.

The Grail
is hidden in
a temple.

Indy and his father must
be careful! There are lots of
dangerous traps and a knight
protecting the Grail.

On another adventure, an evil lady called Irina Spalko wants to find the Crystal Skull of the Lost City of Gold.

She asks Indy for his help. The skull has special powers.

Indy must find the City of Gold. It is hidden in the Amazon rainforest in South America where some native tribes live also.

As Indy and his friends travel through the rainforest they are chased by thousands of killer ants!

In the temple Indy finds more
Crystal Skulls—on Crystal
Skeletons. He discovers that
the Crystal Skeletons are aliens.

The aliens' spaceship rises up
from the temple.

It disappears and the City of
Gold is destroyed.

# Glossary

**Ancient artifacts** (p.4)
Objects that are very old.
They are very interesting
and can be valuable.

**Archaeologist** (p.4)
Someone who studies
the past by finding and
looking at old objects.

**Inflatable** (p.11)
Something that can be
filled with air or gas
and made bigger.

**Trance** (p.17)
Being in a trance is
a bit like being asleep.
A person in a trance
cannot move or act
for themselves.

# Index